BEAN STACK

Written by Laurence Anholt
Illustrated by Arthur Robins

ORCHARD BOOKS

First published in Great Britain in 1996 by Orchard Books
This edition published in 2017 by The Watts Publishing Group

13

Text copyright © Laurence Anholt, 1996
Illustrations copyright © Arthur Robins, 1996

The moral rights of the author and illustrator have been asserted.

A CIP catalogue record for this book
is available from the British Library.

ISBN 978 1 84121 408 5

Printed and bound in Great Britain by
Clays Ltd, St Ives plc

The paper and board used in this book are
made from wood from responsible sources.

MIX
Paper from
responsible sources
FSC® C104740

Orchard Books
An imprint of
Hachette Children's Group
Part of The Watts Publishing Group Limited
Carmelite House
50 Victoria Embankment
London EC4Y 0DZ
An Hachette UK Company
www.hachette.co.uk

www.hachettechildrens.co.uk

☆ Ghostyshocks ☆ Snow White ☆ Cinderboy ☆ Eco-Wolf ☆
☆ The Greedy Farmer ☆ Billy Beast ☆

12

Daft Jack and his mother were so poor...

...they lived under a cow in a field. His mum slept at the front end...

...and Jack slept at the udder end.

Daisy was a good cow, but the problem was, Jack's mum was fed up with milk. It was all they ever had –
hot milk,
cold milk,
warm milk,
milk on toast,
milk pudding.

And on Sundays, for a special treat, they had Milk Surprise (which was really just milk with milk on top).

Jack didn't mind milk, but his mother would have given anything for a change.

"I'M SICK AND TIRED OF MILK!" she would shout. "If I never taste another drop as long as I live it will be too soon. If only you were a clever boy, Jack, you would think of something."

"I have thought of something," said Jack. "It's a new kind of milkshake – it's milk flavoured."

Jack's mum chased him all around the field.

One day, a terrible thing happened; Jack was sitting in the field eating a Mini Milk lolly and his mum was having her after-milk rest when Daisy suddenly looked up at the grey sky, decided it was going to rain and, as all cows do, lay down.

"Right! That is it. I've had enough!" spluttered Jack's mum when Jack had pulled her out by the ankles. "You will have to take Daisy into town and sell her. But make sure you get a good price or I'll chase you around the field for a week."

Daft Jack was very sad because Daisy was more like a friend than just a roof over his head. But he always liked to please his mother.

He made himself a milk sandwich for the journey and Jack and Daisy set off towards the town. It was a long way so they took it in turns to carry each other.

Then at the top of a hill, they met an old
man sitting on a tree stump with a
shopping bag.

"That's a fine cow you're carrying," he said. "What's your name, sonny?"

"It's Jack," said Jack, "but everyone calls me 'Daft', I don't know why."

"Well, Jack," said the old man. "I'd like to buy that cow from you."

"I would like to sell this cow too," said Jack, "but you'll have to give me a good price for her. Otherwise my mum will chase me around the field for a week."

"I can see you're a clever boy," said the old man, "and I'm in a good mood today. So guess what I'm going to give you for that cow?"

"What?" said Jack.

The old man reached into his shopping
bag.

"Beans!" said the old man. "Not just one
bean! Not just two beans! I'm going to give
you A WHOLE TIN OF BAKED BEANS."

Jack couldn't believe his luck. Not one bean, not two beans, but a WHOLE TIN of baked beans for just one old cow. It must have been his lucky day. At last his mum would be proud of him.

So Jack kissed Daisy goodbye and set off home carrying the tin of beans as carefully as he would carry a new born baby, feeling very pleased with himself.

As soon as he saw the field he began to shout, "Look Mum! All our troubles are over. Guess what I got for Daisy? Not one bean. Not two beans. But A WHOLE TIN COMPLETELY FULL OF BEANS! Why, mother there must be A HUNDRED yummy beans in this tin, I knew you'd be pleased."

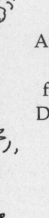

At the end of the week,
when his mum had
finished chasing him,
Daft Jack and his mum
sat down in the
middle of the field.

"Oh Jack," wailed his mum. "Now we haven't even got a cow to sleep under. If only you were a clever boy, you'd think of something."

"I have thought of something, Mum," said Jack. "Let's eat the beans."

So Daft Jack and his mum ate the beans. Then they had nothing left at all.

That night, Jack couldn't sleep. "I can't
do anything right," he thought sadly. "My
poor Mother would be better off without
me. I think I will run away into the big
wide world and seek my fortune."

So Jack decided to leave a note for his mother. He couldn't find any paper so he tore the label from the bean tin. But there was something already written on the back of the baked bean label.

Jack held the paper up to the moonlight and read aloud...

CONGRATULATIONS! You have bought THE LUCKY BEAN TIN and won a FANTASTIC PRIZE for you and your family!

Jack woke his mother. When she saw the message on the bean tin, she couldn't believe her eyes. "Oh Jack!" she cried. "At last we will be able to buy a proper house."

"Yes," said Jack, "and I will buy poor Daisy back. I fancy a nice glass of milk."

And Jack's mum was too happy to chase him around the field.

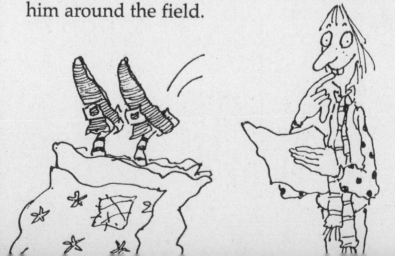

In the morning they sent off the lucky bean label and soon their prize arrived – A WHOLE LORRY LOAD OF BAKED BEANS.

Jack and his mum didn't know what to
say. They began to stack the tins in one
corner of the field, but before they had
finished, a second lorry load of beans
arrived.

And all day long the lorries kept coming. By the evening there was a huge pile of bean tins. A STACK of bean tins. A COLOSSAL GLEAMING MONUMENTAL MOUNTAIN of bean tins. There were bean tins right up to the clouds.

So from that day Daft Jack and his mum ate beans. It was all they ever had –

hot beans,
cold beans,
warm beans,
beans on toast,
bean pudding.

And on Sundays, for a special treat, they had Bean Surprise (which was really just beans with beans on top).

Jack's mum would have given anything for a change.

"I'm SICK AND TIRED OF BEANS!" she shouted one day. "If I never eat another bean as long as I live it will be too soon. If only you were a clever boy, Jack, you would think of something."

"I have thought of something," said Jack.
"Bean juice milkshake."

There wasn't room to chase Jack around the field because the bean stack was too big. So Jack's mum chased him up the bean stack instead.

Higher and higher, Jack hopped from tin to tin with his mum puffing and panting behind.

Until at last Jack climbed so high, he left his mum far behind. But Jack didn't stop. He kept on climbing. He looked down at the world below. He saw the field as small as a handkerchief and his mum as tiny as an ant. And still Jack climbed higher.

When he was almost too tired to climb any more, Jack reached the top of the bean stack, way up in the clouds.

Jack looked around. To his amazement
he saw an enormous castle with its great
door wide open.

He tiptoed inside. It was the most
incredible place he had ever seen.

Jack wandered from room to room. He found massive bedrooms with carpets as thick as snow drifts, a solar heated Jacuzzi, a living room with great armchairs and a TV screen the size of a cinema.

At last, Jack
wandered into a
wonderful kitchen
fitted with every
kind of gadget.

Jack was interested in cooking and he climbed up to look at the giant sized microwave.

Suddenly, the whole castle began to shake. A great voice roared.

Jack looked around in alarm and saw an enormous giant sitting at a table, rubbing his stomach and looking very miserable.

"'S not fair!" complained the giant. "All I ever get to eat is CHILDREN! And now I've got a belly ache...

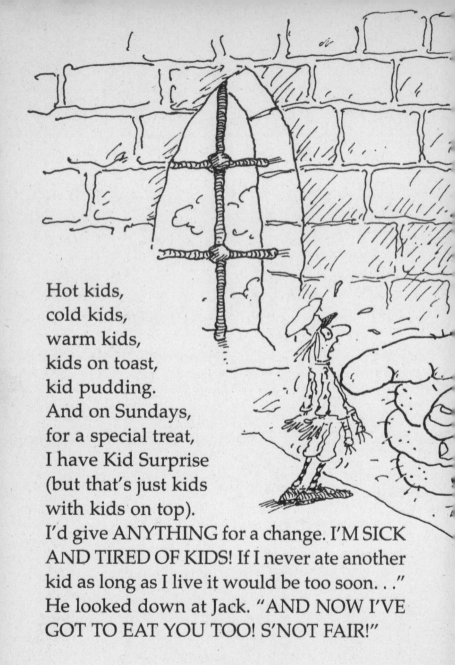

Hot kids,
cold kids,
warm kids,
kids on toast,
kid pudding.
And on Sundays,
for a special treat,
I have Kid Surprise
(but that's just kids
with kids on top).
I'd give ANYTHING for a change. I'M SICK
AND TIRED OF KIDS! If I never ate another
kid as long as I live it would be too soon. . ."
He looked down at Jack. "AND NOW I'VE
GOT TO EAT YOU TOO! S'NOT FAIR!"

The giant reached out a huge hairy hand and grabbed Jack around the waist.

He lifted Jack kicking and struggling into the air and opened his vast black cave-like mouth with a tongue like a huge purple carpet.

"Well," thought Jack, "this is the end of Daft Jack and no mistake."

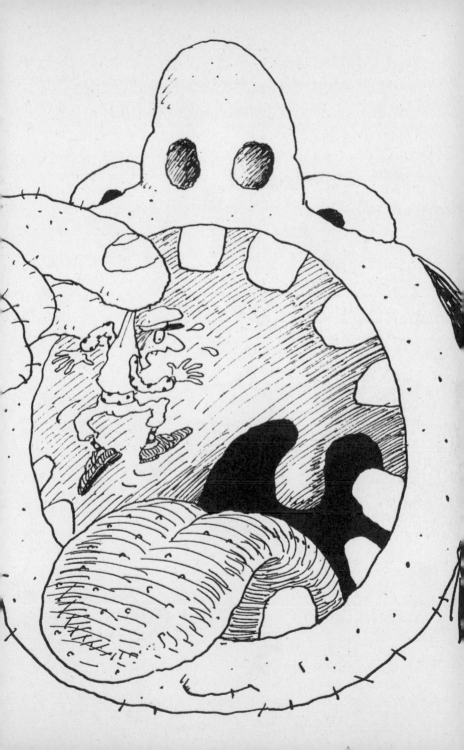

He was just about to be crunched into a
million tiny daft pieces, when suddenly he
had an idea.

"Er, Excuse me, Mr Giant," he whispered nervously. "If you eat me it will only make your tummy ache worse. I can think of something much nicer. I don't suppose you like...beans do you?"

"BEANS!" roared the giant "DO I LIKE BEANS? I YUMMY YUMMY LOVE 'em!"

So Jack took the giant by the hand and led him down the bean stack. And on the way, the giant told Jack how lonely he was, all by himself in the great big castle in the clouds with nothing to do but eat people.

Jack began to feel very sorry for the poor giant and took him home to meet his mum.

"Oh Jack," she cried. "Where ever have you bean?"

Jack's mum was very pleased to see Jack in one piece. But when she saw the giant...!

And when the giant saw Jack's mum...!

It was love at first sight.

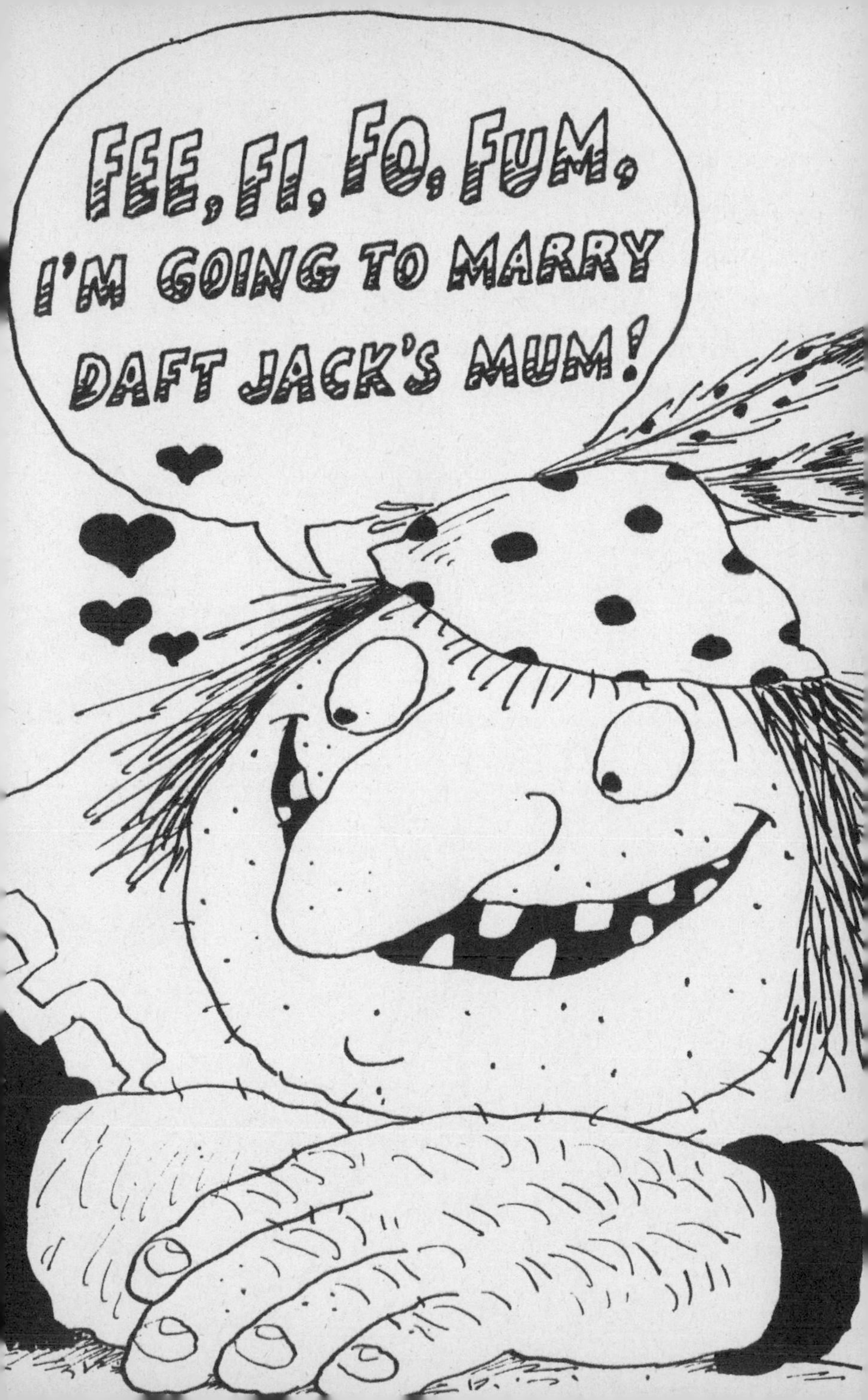
FEE, FI, FO, FUM,
I'M GOING TO MARRY
DAFT JACK'S MUM!

"Of course you are, dear," said Jack's mum, "but first you must be hungry after your long journey."

The giant looked at the bean stack, gleaming in the evening light as he licked his giant lips.

He began munching the beans. Not one tin, not two tins, but the whole stack of beans. And he didn't even stop to open the tins.

So Daft Jack's mum married the giant, and they were very happy. They all went to live in the giant's wonderful castle in the sky.

Daft Jack opened a café in the giant's kitchen and he called it 'DAFT JACK'S SKY SNACKS'. And people came from far and wide and Jack grew rich and happy.

He served everything you can think of except milk...
and beans!